Premier League, We're Having a Laugh!

Managing Chester City in the World's Toughest League

by Jason Whittle

Premier League, We're Having a Laugh!: Managing Chester City in the Highest League

Copyright © 2020 Jason Whittle. All rights reserved.

No part of this book may be reproduced or transmitted in any form or by any means, electronic or mechanical, including photocopying, recording, or by any other information storage and retrieval system without the written permission of the author, except in the case of brief quotations embodied in critical articles and reviews. This book is a work of fiction, all names, characters, places, and events are products of the author's imagination, or are used fictitiously. Any resemblance to actual persons, living or dead, events, or locations is entirely coincidental. Player and team names, and match results, are taken from a simulated season of the vintage computer game, Championship Manager 94.

All rights reserved. Except as permitted under the UK Copyright, Designs and Patents Act 1988.

Chapter 1 – The Off-season

I stepped off the bus; dizzy, euphoric, feeling like I was in a dream. I was soaked in champagne from head to toe; my hair was sticky and sweet, and I could feel bubbles fizzing in my ears and nostrils. It had smeared my glasses too, I thought, but then again my blurred vision could have been because so much of the champagne had found its way into my mouth, and not all of it accidentally. This was us, the staff and players of Chester City Football Club, celebrating the greatest, most incredible miracle in the history of sport: the promotion of our homely little team into the elite, prestigious and challenging world of the FA Premier League. The smallest club ever to climb so high, and not with a multi-millionaire benefactor, not with a big stadium and vast fan base, but just by pulling together, assembling the best talent we could find, and working our socks off day and night.

Winning promotion from Divisions Three to Two in my first season was a tremendous achievement. A further promotion the next season, as champions, was beyond my wildest dreams. But a third promotion in a row, when even mere survival seemed a distant dream, was a pure impossibility, that cannot have happened, that cannot be explained. But happen it did, and after I'd taken my suit to the dry cleaners – asking for as great a miracle as we had achieved if it was ever to be worn again – and finally stopped making bruises on my arm by constantly pinching myself, I would have to face up to the reality of trying to get these shell-shocked, star-struck lads to try to survive in the toughest, most competitive and unforgiving league in world football. After all we'd accomplished, surviving in the top league would be the greatest achievement of all – but failure to do so could not just wipe the smiles off everyone's faces, but leave the club worse off than it had been before we got there.

In fact, I was very worried about the effect promotion would have on the club's finances. Yes, revenues would be increased, but so would wages. Pundits and predictors were saying that one day television payments would number in the multi-millions, but this was far from being the case yet, and a club our size had to work hard to generate revenue, even at this level. And if we were to get relegated – which seemed a near certainty, although I couldn't say so publicly – then the revenue would go down. The wages however, were locked in and irreversible, with clauses and caveats overseen by the agents and attorneys who had suddenly taken an interest in our players. The salaries would remain high, and it would be very difficult for us to sustain such a financial burden outside of the Premier League. So instead of being a happy go lucky season of fantasy football where we'd be grateful for every single point, there was genuine pressure on us to somehow stay out of the bottom three in a division where we were – by far! – the biggest underdogs *ever* to compete at this level. There was every likelihood the dream could turn into a nightmare.

As expected, when we returned for pre-season, almost everyone in the squad was demanding a hefty pay rise, with the only two exceptions being Steve Lomas and Deryn Brace, who had been at Premier League clubs previously. As much danger as it might have put the club into, playing hardball and refusing the increases wholesale was never really a viable option. To stand any chance of competing, we'd need our team spirit to be stronger than ever: we simply could not afford to go out on the pitch with unhappy players. But I couldn't go throwing money at any or all of our squad, and only those who had contributed significantly to our promotion campaign could honestly say they deserved it. Young players on the fringes of the first team would get the chance to earn that pay increase, but would have to prove themselves worthy of it first. To that end I made most of them available for loan, and Mick Gooding, who at 38 was unlikely to find much improvement, available for a free transfer. As for those I was offering pay rises to, most were sensible and took salaries of between £1,500 and £2,000 a week, but Scott Houghton was alone in demanding more, holding out for over £3,000 a week before he agreed to stay. To be honest, I wasn't happy with the way he conducted himself, and he would have to deliver on the pitch if I was to keep him on the wage bill. And with Southampton and Middlesbrough reported to be interested in signing him, I would consider any offers upwards of £2 million, which Premier League or not, was like lottery win money to a club of our size. The only other irritant on the wage bill was third choice goalkeeper Frank Lee, newly promoted from the youth team. He was a promising prospect, Ireland youth international, but was put straight onto first team wages without me being consulted. I tried to loan him out to get him off the wage bill: Colchester were in for him after their regular keeper Nathan Munson broke his leg – he got Munsoned, all right! – but they pulled out at the last minute, presumably as soon as they realised just how much his services would cost them. Ironically it was our old keeper and club legend Billy Stewart they eventually brought in.

But for all my talk of moving players out, strengthening the squad was all important, but with a total transfer budget in the region of £600,000 it meant I would still be bargain hunting. One way of doing that was to give ageing players their final hurrah, and in a moment of high sentimentality, I dreamed of bringing Vinnie Jones, Stuart Rimmer, or even Ian Rush back here to play for us in the Premier League. More pragmatically, I considered a move for Southampton's Northern Ireland target man Iain Dowie, available for a mere £100,000 and still with something to offer at the age of 31. But to have a chance of recouping future transfer funds, I turned my attention to younger players whose careers had gone in the wrong direction. One candidate was Brighton's Jason Lee, who had been in personal dispute with the club, and had been racked with low morale and hostility from the fans. But he had still scored 28 goals in two seasons, and was also available for just £100,000. However, when I saw that Julian Joachim was available for a couple of hundred thousand, I knew it was him I wanted. He'd been something of a wonderkid at Leicester, tipped for the very top, but instead he'd become something of a footballing nomad. After failing to fulfil his potential at Leicester, he moved to Bristol City, and been excellent there, but a further move to QPR had been a disastrous flop as they slid to rock bottom in Division One. Now he was looking for his fourth club in as many seasons, and I was keen for us to be that club. Not that I said so, of course. I came in low and hopeful at £150,000, before eventually doing the deal at £190,000. If he could replicate his Bristol City form, it would be a very good deal: if he could live up to his early promise, it would be an incredible one.

The only other signing was one which gave me an instant feeling of buyer's remorse: Des Seaman, a left sided defender or midfielder from Bristol Rovers, who had done well in a handful of appearances the season before, and at only 19 years of age, had the potential to develop and be worth many times the £20,000 outlay. But I brought him in on Premier League wages, as I would have to for every new signing, and I found myself second guessing the decision to pay such a high salary for what was essentially a third choice squad backup who might not even take to the pitch at all in competitive action. Perhaps it was a signing best made only when circumstances such as injury or suspension demanded it. But in any case, the deal was done, although higher profile left sided options such as Trevor Sinclair, John Salako or Paul Peschisolido remained on my radar. But for now, I would be going into pre-season with two new faces, and a cool £400,000 still in the transfer kitty.

Chapter 2 – Pre-season:

With a few new faces in the squad, and plenty more with something to prove, I scheduled in a full programme of seven friendlies, with the first choice line-up playing on Saturdays, and the fringe players being given midweek run-outs. The Saturday squad would start at Hull for a reunion with Stuart Rimmer, followed by a nice trip to the seaside to play Brighton, a home game against Sheffield Wednesday, newly relegated from the Premier League, and an even nicer trip to the seaside to face Cannes. The second string were given home fixtures, and local ones, against Crewe, Wrexham and Stockport, to give them a taste of reasonably competitive action – since no local derby can be truly friendly – inside the Deva Stadium.

However, on the eve of our first friendly, a couple of injuries in training set back my plans, and blurred the lines between the two squads a bit. Losing Ian Bennett wasn't the worst thing, as it would allow me to compare my other two goalkeepers, but losing Julian Joachim for most of pre-season was a blow, as that was his chance to settle in a bit before the league season.

So we went to Hull with Frank Lee taking the gloves, and Andy Curtis restored to the number 8 shirt and the captain's armband. It was neither a great match nor a vintage performance, but we did enough to take a workmanlike 1-0 win, which would have been more comfortable if not for Scott Houghton missing yet another penalty. But nobody disgraced themselves, nobody shone through, and Paul Stephenson's goal was enough to give us the win. Stuart Rimmer came on as sub for the hosts, which surprised me as I thought he'd be their star striker, but he showed enough against us to prove he still has something to offer. Hull's subsequent, audacious swoop for Guy Whittingham pushed him further down the pecking order, but I can't help thinking what a great partnership they'd make; both experienced, both predatory, both still quite pacy, and the classic big man, little man combination.

The experimental squad kicked off their pre-season at home to Crewe, and they too ground out a 1-0 win, although it took a last-minute penalty save by Don Chambers to preserve it. The other youngsters to impress me were Ian Jackson, who took his goal really well, and above all Don Hopkin, who produced an eye-catching performance of assuredness and maturity at the back. At the other end of the age and performance scale, Mick Gooding seriously struggled, and it looked like this would be a season too far for him, and certainly at Premier League level.

I took the lads down to Brighton next, for a few days down by the sea which they so richly deserved, with wives and girlfriends welcome. Sure it was Travelodge rather than the Grand Hotel, but the players could relax and unwind by the sea, take their loved ones shopping on The Lanes, and the few with children could take them to the beach or the amusement arcades. And we all bonded further with a day at the horse racing – albeit nowhere near as good a course as the one we have back in Chester – and an evening going on a gothic ghost walk tour. There was still work to be done on the pitch though, and done it was, with a satisfyingly professional performance and a comfortable 2-0 win. Our right side pairing of Andy Thomson and Scott Houghton were particularly strong, both getting on the scoresheet, and Paul Stephenson was a constant threat up front. Iain Jenkins and Mark Limbert didn't have great games at the back, but their mistakes went unpunished because Jason Lee was ineffective up front for the hosts. I don't know if he realised he was playing his way out of a potential move to the Premier League, but I cooled my interest based on that performance, and declined to intervene when he ended up moving to Watford instead. In fairness, he'd probably do a decent job for them, but there must have been a lot of regret around Vicarage Road about letting Bruce Dyer go.

It was cross border derby day against Wrexham for the shadow squad next, to give them a taste of the big match atmosphere, and a game with a bit of an edge. It was another clean sheet and another win, 1-0 with Ian Jackson again on the scoresheet and Don Hopkin again excellent in defence, although we were helped by Wrexham having a goal disallowed in the second half. Welshman Deryn Brace put in a quality performance against his compatriots, and a half-fit Julian Joachim came through unscathed to shake off some rust. I played him up front instead of midfield, to keep him away from Vinnie, because last season playing for QPR, Julian had put a bad challenge on Vinnie, and friendly or not, I wouldn't have put it past our erstwhile captain to go looking for revenge. Maybe he was just in a good mood though, and he had every reason to be, because he told me after the game that he'd been cast in his first movie role. He was in a British gangster film playing an East End hardman, which I guess he'd been preparing for through method acting all his life, and sure enough the diver called Jason something got a part in it too. Vinnie said he'd get me on the guest list for the premiere; another reason I was glad to have stayed in touch with him, but still I doubted that it would be a lavish, star-studded affair.

Next up was what I saw as the most important of the pre-season friendlies, at home to Sheffield Wednesday, who had been relegated from the Premier League the season before, making it a good yardstick for our survival chances. So I was hugely disappointed that we put in such a lacklustre display, hardly creating a chance in our 1-0 loss, often conceding possession too cheaply, and with not one single player putting in a performance they could be proud of. We still might have scraped a draw, but Scott Houghton missed yet another penalty – probably the last one he'll take for a while – but in fairness we were well beaten, and deserved no more than we got.

It was back to winning ways for the second string though, perhaps sensing potential first team opportunities now, That said, it was only a couple players with plenty of senior experience who really staked their claims in Deryn Brace and Andy Curtis, although Don Hopkin was rock solid once again. And it was great to see Julian Joachim continue his rehabilitation with his first goal in a Chester City shirt; and even better that it should come from the spot, which my players often made look like an impossible task! The only question marks were at full back, with my impulse buy Des Seaman on the left doing little to justify his signing, and on the right not actually a question mark at all but a definitive answer on Mick Gooding, who sadly is just no longer anywhere near the standard required at this level: even in the event of an injury crisis I would be best off trying someone else out of position.

The final pre-season fixture was the chairman's reward for our achievements, and the glitziest away trip yet: to Cannes! We'd missed the film festival by about ten weeks, but it was still a level of glamour unprecedented for a club who hitherto played friendlies at Goole, Glossop North End, and North Ferriby United. It was a morale building trip, a team bonding one, and a treat for all concerned. But it was still a working trip, with fitness and technical training to be done, and a really challenging fixture against a team in France's top flight.

Paul Stephenson picked up a knock in training, so Julian Joachim slotted in up front alongside Bruce Dyer, who had endured a barren pre-season thus far. Andy Thomson was feeling a slight hamstring tightness too, so Deryn Brace, who had looked in good nick, came into the side at right back. Both played their part in an excellent performance, a thrilling performance, the complete performance. And Bruce Dyer emerged just in time for the new season, weighing in with two trademark goals: a rasping drive from the edge of the box, and a thumping header from a Scott Houghton cross. We had defenders getting in on the goal action too, Iain Jenkins and Mark Limbert both scoring to secure a magnificent 4-0 win. Only Alexei Poddubski was slightly below his best, but Nicky Southall, now well down the pecking order since Joachim's arrival, came on and showed that he still has something to offer. It all went to show that we still had some depth to the squad, the lads were hitting form just at the right time, and despite being fully aware of the size of the task before us, and what a monumental effort it would acquire to finish anywhere other than rock bottom, we went into the league campaign brimming with confidence.

Chapter 3 – August:

We returned from Cannes to a little bit of transfer business, and a couple of outgoings. Firstly, Yeovil came in for young Steve Harrison on loan, and I was happy for him to go off and get some first team experience there. You certainly couldn't expect him to force his way into a Premier League side at the age of 17, and Don Hopkin's impressive pre-season performances had clearly marked him as the next one in line to challenge for a place in the starting XI. I was looking for the other move to be a loan too, one of our backup goalkeepers, but when Crewe came in for Don Chambers, it was for a permanent move instead – that penalty save in the friendly must have made quite an impression!

    I didn't really want to let him go on a permanent transfer, but we couldn't block the move because his contract on Division Two wages had expired, and I was holding fire on offering a Premier League one. So he was on his way out one way or the other, and the fee would go to a tribunal if we couldn't agree it: I managed to bump the fee up to £200,000; it was good money for an untried youngster, it gave us a little bit more clout in the transfer market, and stopped us being overburdened in the position.

Ironic therefore, that we went so suddenly from having three keepers to only one: Ian Bennett broke a rib in training, and would be out for two months. As it stood, instead of going on loan to Colchester, Frank Lee was in line to make his Premier League debut. Only I really didn't think we could afford that. If we were to have any chance of survival, we needed a solid start, and exposing a novice goalie to a potential drubbing was something from which we might be unable to recover.

Fortunately, the duration of Ian Bennett's time out injured was the same as that of the standard loan move. I went into the market for the best one we could find, and was pleasantly surprised to find Chelsea's Russian international stopper Dimitri Kharine available, having been one of the very best keepers in the Premier League the previous season, but in a surprise move Chelsea had signed Jan Stejskal from Portsmouth and installed him as their first choice number one. I hoped he'd do well for them, not least because I didn't want Chelsea changing their minds and recalling Kharine before Ian Bennett recovered. But it was worth the risk and the near £5,000 weekly salary to get him between the sticks.

His first game would be at Blackburn, an intimidating opener for our first game at this level, but made less daunting by the home side's catastrophic summer departures: Paul Warhurst, Graeme Le Saux, and worst, Alan Shearer all leaving to play on the continent. It might be a good time for us to meet them, before they had a chance to rebuild. We ourselves would be without Iain Jenkins for the opener, a suspension held over from last season, but Graham Potter would fill in at left back. It should have been the catalyst for Des Seaman to claim a place on the bench, but I couldn't trust him enough, and Deryn Brace and Julian Joachim had done enough against Cannes to consider themselves unlucky not to be starting, never mind getting a place in the squad.

We started quite well, keeping it even for ten minutes, and then there was an incident which changed the perspective of the game. Blackburn's Neil Heaney, taking Alan Shearer's old place in the side, hit Paul Stephenson with a rash, dangerous challenge which took him out of the game. I was seething, having lost a key man and expecting the offender to get away with it, but Heaney was shown a straight red. Suddenly, with Julian Joachim coming on for his debut far earlier than he could have imagined, we were in a strong position to get something out of the game.

But the atmosphere was charged and tempers were fraying, and Andy Thomson was incredibly fortunate to escape with a yellow card after appearing to put his head in on Kevin Gallagher during a scuffle. And Blackburn had the first clear chance, but fortunately for us it fell to right back Patrik Andersson, and his effort was dependably dealt with by Kharine. Jim Magilton was the next man booked, for a foul on Poddubski, but still Blackburn were forging the better openings, even with ten men, Tim Sherwood the next to spurn a clear cut chance, and we made it to half time with the scores level. Graham Potter was struggling at left back, but we had no direct replacement, and only one change left after the injury, so I let him continue.

On the hour we picked up our second booking, Steve Lomas with a heavy challenge on Jason Wilcox, but still it was 11 v 10 in our favour, and just as well, because it was a hard enough game even still. And on 73 minutes, the breakthrough finally came, Tim Sherwood atoning for his earlier miss, to give the home side the lead.

Suddenly we had to attack. I brought Brace on for Potter and threw Scott Houghton up front in a 3-4-3 formation, but it didn't yield any clear chances, and we went down to a 1-0 defeat despite playing against ten men for most of the game. It served to outline just how hard it will be in this league. Needless to say, the chants of "Going down!" and, "Premier League! You're having a laugh!" came cascading down from the stands. I expected to hear a lot of that sort of thing; we had been ever since we clinched promotion, to be honest.

The game was swiftly followed by two more loan approaches: both were to players not far from the first team, and both were welcome. Don Hopkin moved to Division Two side Leyton Orient, looking to see if he could turn his impressive pre-season form into some competitive league performances, and we allowed a more experienced player to leave too. After 116 appearances and 12 goals for us, Nicky Southall shouldn't have had too much left to prove, but I was looking to get him off the wage bill for a while, and give him a first team run I couldn't promise here. So I let him go to Kettering in Division Three, and hoped to have him eventually come back full of confidence. Both of these lads moving out would be star players for their temporary clubs if they played to their full potential.

Our next match was a special one in various ways. Above all, as our first ever home game in the Premier League, but also a momentous occasion for me against Southampton, my boyhood club. Throw in the fact that they were the league leaders following their 3-0 win over Millwall on opening day, and it got bigger still. And we needed something out of it; the longer we stayed on zero points, the more people would start to accept our relegation as an inevitability.

We were hampered by the loss of Alexei Poddubski to a twisted ankle picked up against Blackburn, that would most likely keep him out at the weekend too. This would put Graham Potter back in the side, and I was hoping to see an improvement in his performance.

In front of a record crowd and in a pulsating atmosphere, we competed well in the first half, bossing the midfield, but without creating any notable chances. Until the 40th minute, when skipper Andy Curtis timed his run from midfield to get behind the defence and finish in style. He was finally putting my doubts about signing him firmly to bed. 1-0 to Chester at half time.

Five minutes into the second half, the next big chance fell to Graham Potter who was getting time and space from Chris Stewart, a left back filling in out of place on the right, and struggling to adapt. Potter dragged his shot wide, but I hoped he'd get another chance. But after a quiet spell, it was Curtis who got the chance, with 12 minutes remaining. He shifted the ball to give himself a yard of space on his right foot, and it was all he needed to whip a wicked, curling shot into the top corner. An excellent strike, 2-0, with both goals by the captain, and more importantly, three priceless points within touching distance.

Saints made immediate changes, but I was shocked and relieved to see Matt Le Tissier substituted, with them bringing on Paul Simpson and Dean Saunders, while probably looking to play a bit more direct. But it brought nothing as we held on doggedly but assuredly, to claim a famous win. And with that we rose into mid table, and Andy Curtis, the signing I'd second guessed, and who Julian Joachim was expected to replace, was now joint top scorer in the Premier League.

It was good that we had three points on the board, because we had an intimidating fixture next up: away to Manchester United. But it would be a great celebratory occasion for us too, with almost as many fans as we can fit in the Deva Stadium making the relatively short journey to Old Trafford. And while we were undoubtedly huge underdogs, we went there as the higher placed team in the league, following United's disappointing start of one draw and one loss.

Needless to say, the most important thing there was to avoid conceding the early goal. That's easier said than done though, and we buckled to the early pressure after just ten minutes, Dion Dublin cracking United into the lead. At least we consolidated after that though, and went in at half time just the one goal behind. We should have been dead and buried ten minutes into the second half though. Roy Keane sprang from midfield with just Kharine to beat, took it round him, but only found the side netting with the goal gaping. I tried to capitalise on the let off by adopting a more positive mentality; Graham Potter freed from the thankless task of trying to contain Ryan Giggs, and given licence to get forward as a winger. And a few minutes later we worked an opportunity for Paul Stephenson, but he sent his effort the wrong side of the post.

With the game approaching the last fifteen minutes, Dion Dublin took out Iain Jenkins with an ugly, scything challenge. It had to be a red card, had to be, but bigger clubs than ourselves have been on the wrong end of many a decision there, and so it proved again; Dublin getting away with a yellow as Jenkins was stretchered off. I brought on Joachim in his place anyway, and decided to go for broke in the time remaining. We launched something of a late onslaught, but nothing came of it, and we went down to another 1-0 defeat. No disgrace, but no points either.

At least with no midweek fixture, we had a week to patch up the walking wounded, and were expected to be fit and firing for the visit of Tottenham Hotspur. They sat rock bottom after a nightmare start of three defeats out of three, and we'd beaten them twice at home in going up with them last season, but this was still a David and Goliath clash: a draw would be a great result.

What we did have in midweek, instead of a game, was a massive boost from international call ups, the biggest shock being Frank Lee's first call up to the *full* Ireland squad. And he'd get his chance with us in the League Cup soon enough. He was joined by Liam Daish in the Irish squad, and Deryn Brace kept his place in the Wales squad.

Furthermore, and so promising for the future, we were by far the biggest contributors to the England Under-21 squad, with four players picked, when no other side had more than one. And there was some degree of personal pride too, in seeing Andy Thomson, Don Hopkin, Steve Lomas, and Bruce Dyer all donning the Three Lions. For Hopkin especially it was a meteoric rise, from nowhere to a seriously hot prospect in just a few weeks. I actually wished there was a clearer route into our first team for him.

There was nearly a calamitous beginning for us against Spurs, as our former loanee Nick Barmby was left all alone in the box after only three minutes, but he got his finish all wrong. The game went a bit stale from there, and we reached half time level before a new record attendance, but we were always second best.

Andy Curtis was having an off day, but he threw them in occasionally, and I was learning to take the rough with the smooth with him; on his day he was one of our best. More concerning was our weakness on left, Iain Jenkins and Alexei Poddubski both struggling.

Spurs took the lead eight minutes after half time, and as I feared, it came down our left, with Darren Anderton getting on the scoresheet. Graham Potter's recent performances hadn't really justified a place on the bench, so I had to leave them on, but I replaced Andy Curtis with Julian Joachim, giving him free licence to maraud forward. I also brought on Deryn Brace to bomb forward like an auxiliary winger from right back. But still we couldn't muster a worthwhile chance, and slumped to yet another 1-0 defeat.

We were still above the relegation zone, but only just, and it was clear we had two major problems, even taking as read that we were out of our depth at this level. Firstly, we weren't scoring enough goals. There wasn't much I could do about that, at least not yet. We were already playing two up front, against the sage advice of many a pundit, and we had some creativity in midfield. I would keep plugging away with what we had for a couple more games yet, and hope that goals would come without drastic action being taken.

But drastic action *was* required on the left, where our weakness was being exploited, and costing us precious points. Other sides would notice that, and look to attack us there, so something had to be done. I still believed that Iain Jenkins was the man to wear our number 3 shirt long term, albeit on rotten current form, but there were major doubts as to whether Alexei Poddubski and Graham Potter were capable of playing in the Premier League. It had also become clear that I'd got it badly wrong in signing Des Seaman, who in reality added no depth at all to the squad, because he put no pressure on the incumbents, nor could he be trusted to fill in for them while they were injured or off form. But I tried not to dwell on that, annoyed at myself as I was – not at him, it wasn't his fault – because it was more important right now to bring someone in who could have a positive effect.

Fortunately, I had just the man in mind – Tony Thomas. He'd bring quality and strength to left back or left midfield, and having just won his first full cap he was full of confidence. Sadly we couldn't afford to buy him outright, but another loan move, after his successful spell with us last season, would give him the taste of Premier League football he craved, would be a move he could make without leaving home, and from Tranmere's point of view would keep the sharks looking to sign him permanently at bay for a while. This was how I pitched it to them; fortunately they agreed, and the deal was done. We needed him badly, as we began our second month in the Premier League.

Chapter 4 – September:

Tony Thomas would be making his debut away to Arsenal at Highbury, another fiendishly difficult fixture, and my dilemma was where to play him. My first thought was to bring Thomas in at left back, and take Jenkins out of the firing line for a bit, keeping him on the bench to regain his confidence with a run out from the bench. But that would have left no room in the dugout for Julian Joachim, the only potential game changer we had to bring on. So I changed things around again – I don't know if it was genius or madness to change the starting eleven to accommodate who'd be on the bench, but I plumped for Jenkins at left back, with Thomas ahead of him hopefully being a reassuring factor who would help him get his game back. Joachim and Brace would be the boys on the bench, Potter would be the latest offered out on loan, and Poddubski's turn would come. It was the best balance we could find; I just had to hope it was a combination which would yield some points.

    I began to believe it might as we acquitted ourselves solidly early on. And then, 26 minutes on the clock, a half clearance falls to Andy Curtis. A solid strike on the half volley, the ball screaming past David Seaman's outstretched fingers, smashing off the underside of the bar and into the back of the net. What a goal! What a goal, what an impact Curtis was having on the Premier League, and what a chance to pick up our first away points in the top flight.

We held our lead comfortably for all of two minutes, before Martin Keown rose highest from a corner and thundered a header goalwards, only for Kharine to turn it away spectacularly. But just one minute later they were back at us again. This time the chance fell to Paul Merson, and he made no mistake with an exquisite lob for the equaliser. We'd awaken the beast and were paying for it, and Liam Daish was enduring a torrid time at the back. At least we found a foothold after that, with the left side pairing working particularly well, and we took it in at half time with scores level.

At the start of the second half, a Mark Limbert howler let in David Hillier. He took it round Kharine and looked set to slot it in to the empty net, but for an excellent recovery sprint from Iain Jenkins to clear off the line and justify my faith in him. We were living on borrowed time though, and I had to make a change, and a reshuffle.

Deryn Brace in on the right, Scott Houghton into the middle, and Steve Lomas dropping back.

With eight minutes remaining, Arsenal brought Ian Wright on, and went with three up front. I pulled Deryn Brace back to sweeper, moved Scott Houghton back to the right, and left any counter attacking duties to Tony Thomas, since they no longer had a right winger to threaten him with. But I knew we'd be under a bombardment, and we so nearly saw it through, but in the last minute Eddie McGoldrick went down in the box, the North Bank howled for a penalty, and the ref bowed to the pressure and pointed to the spot.

My heart sank, and I braced myself to try and lift the lads after our most hurtful defeat yet. Ian Wright stepped up, slotted it to the keeper's left, and Kharine flew across the goal to turn it away and behind! Even as I jumped up and down, celebrating like crazy in front of the dugout, I still found myself remembering the end of *Escape to Victory*. Maybe they'd remake that, with Vinnie as the star.

Our ordeal wasn't over yet though. From the resultant corner, Martin Keown went down, claiming *another* penalty! My heart was in my mouth as the ref put the whistle to his lips, but thankfully it was to blow for full time. A 1-1 draw, a single point, but one of the most emotional moments of my career. The lads went the whole length of the pitch, from the penalty area where we'd been camped out, to behind the Arsenal goal, so we could celebrate with our supporters. This was a special result, this was a special night, this was for the fans. They would be getting home in the early hours of the morning, and every one of them would feel it's worth it. They would remember this night for the rest of their lives, show their grandchildren the matchday programme, and say that they were there. This is why I love this game.

High flying Newcastle would provide a stern test on their visit a few days later, and we might be carrying some fatigue, but I took the massive morale boost to overcome that, and intended to name an unchanged side. In fact the only player whose morale was a concern was Ian Bennett. He was in physical pain, frustrated at not playing, had had to delay the Premier League debut he'd been dreaming of, and now had to watch on as his temporary replacement lapped up all the adulation and hero worship. I hoped he could raise his spirits before his return to the side, or it might adversely affect his performances.

In the meantime we had a key clash with Newcastle to get through, a side with so many attacking options that Teddy Sheringham was likely to start on the bench, behind Alex Mathie and Andy Cole, who was rumoured to have such an acrimonious relationship with Sheringham that the two never spoke, and took opposite ends of the dressing room. Whatever their dynamic was, Dimitri Kharine was likely to be busy again.

We had a setback in the opening seconds when Andy Thomson was booked for a foul on Alex Mathie. A bit harsh for a first offence I thought, and it meant he had a long time to get through without offending again. And then Mathie punished us further, much more severely, when he got on the end of the resulting free kick to bundle the ball home. 1-0 down, and still in the very first minute! A nightmare start!

The game quietened down after that, with hardly a chance on either side, but five minutes before half time Nicky Papavasilou evaded Thomson – perhaps reluctant to make the challenge – and broke clear. He rounded Kharine smartly to make it 2-0 and leave us with a mountain to climb.

I went for broke at half time, making both substitutions, and changing the mentality of the team. Deryn Brace replaced Thomson at right back, Joachim came on for Lomas in midfield, and all full backs and midfielders were urged to push on and attack.

Mathie could have walked ten minutes into the second half, for what looked like an elbow on Mark Limbert, but he was very fortunate to escape with a yellow card, and the injustice was compounded with 18 minutes to go, as Steve Potts added a third. And that was how it stayed, a crushing 3-0 home defeat, just when I thought we were finding our feet in this division, and worse, it was a result that dropped us into the bottom three. It made our next match, away to bottom side Millwall, our most important of the season so far.

Before that, we had the distraction of a League Cup draw, and a very welcome distraction it proved to be, with a two-legged double dose of cross border rivalry served up with a game against Wrexham. Two wins over our local rivals would reinforce bragging rights for the foreseeable future, and provide a welcome boost to all at the club.

With spirits raised, we went down to capital for the second time in as many weeks, hoping once again we could travel back in celebratory mood. The one thing we couldn't afford to do in that bear pit atmosphere, with their high intensity long ball game, was to fall behind early. And after 11 minutes, that was exactly what we did, inexcusably leaving Darren Simkin alone from a corner, and he made no mistake. Just two minutes later, Mike Jeffrey weighed in with their second, and it looked like the game, and probably our entire season, was sinking fast.

And if there was any doubt that this wasn't our day, it was confirmed after 27 minutes. Andy Curtis went down in the box, and the ref bravely gave a penalty against the hostile crowd. Bruce Dyer stepped up to score his first Premier League goal, and give us a lifeline into the game, but instead hoofed it wildly over the bar and into that ecstatic, braying Millwall crowd.

Half time came and I reprised my substitutions from the last game, Brace and Joachim on for Thomson and Lomas. Neither of the departing players were likely to keep their place. And Joachim had a chance to score with his very first touch, perhaps should have, but fired wide when well placed. But the other sub *did* have his finishing boots on, Deryn Brace marauding into the box and providing an excellent finish. 2-1, and game on! We were rampant now, and on 73 minutes Andy Curtis, now our main danger man this season, strode into the box to slot home an excellent finish and bring us level.

Now it was a game of stick or twist – should we push forward and go all out for the win we deserved, and risk our epic comeback being for nothing? Or settle for what we had and celebrate the result, even if it didn't lift us out of the bottom three?

Millwall blinked first, and that made up my mind. Needing the win even more than we did, they threw on a third striker and left their left side open, and I responded by pulling back, deploying a sweeper, but looking to counter attack down our right through Scott Houghton if they got too careless in their desperation.

But no sooner had the changes been made than Millwall were awarded a penalty, and this time Kharine could do nothing as the spot kick was lashed past him. Now we were chasing again, and I threw everyone forward. And with the very last kick of the game, all hope fading away, Bruce Dyer got behind the defence and produced a beautiful, deft finish into the far corner. 3-3! What a finish! What a game! He'd atoned for his penalty miss, and ensured that once again we'd be heading back north breathless and elated after some stunning late drama. Two score draws that both felt like epic wins.

When the dust settled on that result – and I tried not to get too bogged down on thinking, really, we should have won – we had another massive occasion to look forward to: a minnows v sharks local derby at home to Everton, the sort of fixture that makes you want to pinch yourself to check that it's real.

Steve Lomas's loss of form should have been Alexei Poddubski's ticket back into the starting line-up, in the middle instead of on the left, but a minor, albeit very ill-timed injury kept him out of contention. So instead I went with Julian Joachim in midfield, along with Brace coming in for Thomson. I'd be starting with the same eleven who finished against Millwall, with the two dropped players filling the bench. It would mean a more attack minded centre midfield than I'd usually go with, but I just had to trust them to battle hard and not get overrun.

I thought Joachim would be called upon to take a penalty in the eighth minute, but the referee was the only person in the stadium not to see a clear foul on Bruce Dyer. But the ref did even worse by us midway through the first half. Paul Stephenson beat the offside trap, rounded the keeper and slotted home, only for play to be called back for a late tackle on Andy Curtis after he'd played the through ball, with the ref failing to play the advantage. And it got completely ridiculous on 35 minutes when Scott Houghton was sent off, a straight red for an innocuous challenge on Billy Kenny. It was the worst refereeing performance I'd ever seen; bordering on being distinctly suspicious. But miraculously, with all that was going against us, we went in ahead, with Andy Curtis flicking home Dyer's knockdown to give us the most unlikely, but well-deserved half time lead.

Four minutes after the break, Billy Kenny breached our back line with a late run into the box, but he put his shot wide. I feared it wouldn't be the last chance they had against us, and that it might be time to lose one of our strikers. Tony Thomas had moved to patrol in front of the back four, but in doing that we yielded both flanks to Everton. As we approached the hour mark I was deciding which striker to retain, and was leaning towards Paul Stephenson, when he proved me right by unleashing Stephenson's Rocket, past Jon Sheffield's despairing dive, and into the top corner for a sublime second. Get in!

Rightly or wrongly, that was the cue for me to shut up shop. Steve Lomas came on for Dyer and played sweeper, with Thomas holding on the left, Curtis holding on the right, and Joachim leading any counter attacks to join Stephenson. I hoped it would be enough to hold a two goal lead for half an hour, even with ten men.

It took the Toffees until ten minutes from time to make a change, and even then it was a straight swap up front. But they had nothing to trouble us, and we held on comfortably for another famous win, overcoming such difficulties that it was named performance of the week, not just for the Premier League, but across all four divisions. Most importantly, it lifted us out of the relegation zone, ahead of our cup tie local derby at Wrexham.

Having had performance of the week, and been on the right side of a local derby upset, we had to guard against it going the other way the next game. It wasn't so long ago we'd have been the underdogs for this one, they were still the bigger club, and would fancy their chances of inflicting a humiliation on us here. So that, along with knowing how much this fixture means to the fans, was why I declined to rest players and experiment with our line-up. It was all business for this one, and I wanted to win.

Besides, there were three enforced changes to make anyway. The players on loan, Kharine and Thomas, were unavailable for cup ties, and Scott Houghton had a one match ban to serve after his sending off. It meant we could give a debut to Frank Lee in goal, and recalls to Andy Thomson and Alexei Poddubski to re-stake their claims to a regular first team place.

But in the event, the local derby was, well, a non-event. Wrexham set their stall out with two experienced, tough tackling holding midfielders, former Portsmouth hardman Martin Kuhl and my old mate Vinnie Jones shielding the back four. Consequently we enjoyed long periods of pressure and possession without creating any clear cut chances, perhaps missing the extra guile of Scott Houghton in midfield. With ten minutes to go, Wrexham finally gambled and threw an extra man up front. I could have fought fire with fire and gone all out for the win, but the consequences of defeat would have been unbearable, and a home second leg put us in a strong position. So we took the 0-0 draw, with the shortest ever highlight reel, and moved on to October, and a league game away to surprise early leaders, Ipswich Town.

Chapter 5 – October:

Our first game of the new month was away to a side in good form, but I was confident we could get something out of it. Ipswich aren't the most attack minded sides out there, and they wouldn't blow us away. I thought we could get a foothold in the game and really compete. Thus it was for 20 minutes, and then a sublime piece of poaching from Paul Stephenson gave us a shock lead, ghosting in at the far post from Houghton's low cross. Ipswich almost hit back immediately, Chris Kiwomya outpacing the defence to bear down on Kharine's goal, but he stroked his finish the wrong side of the post, and we took it to half time with our one goal lead intact.

On the hour, Kiwomya got another chance, and this time he found the finish, to level at 1-1. Liam Daish wasn't coping with his movement at all, so I brought him off for the slightly quicker Steve Lomas to come in and take over. Ipswich threw an extra man up front, we covered that and looked for the counter-attack, but I was happy to take yet another away draw – that made it four in a row. And it was another away game next, fairly local, but I didn't know whether to call it a six pointer or not. It was against reigning champions Manchester City, who had been below us after a terrible start, but had leapfrogged us on their current run of four wins in a row, with no goals conceded. Suffice to say, I'd be satisfied with another draw.

Ian Bennett returned to training following his rib injury, but it was too soon to consider him for first team play, and I'd secured Kharine's services for a further month. And even though Andy Thomson was disgruntled at being left out, I'd be going into the Man City match with an unchanged starting line-up and bench.

I thought we'd gone behind on ten minutes when Stefan Beinlich smashed home from the edge of the box, but this time the decision worked in our favour, a slight foul as they won possession being enough to rule out the goal. But we were clearly struggling in midfield, with Tony Thomas and Andy Curtis looking particularly shaky. Moments later, Beinlich again, this time it counted, but thankfully, this time he missed. We were living on borrowed time it seemed.

22 minutes in, *again* Stefan Beinlich, but again the ref helping us, as he went down in the box, the players and fans

appealed, but the referee was unmoved. But City finally took the lead on 34 minutes, this time a trademark bullet header from Niall Quinn. I reacted instantly, taking off Curtis, who was playing an absolute stinker, and giving Joachim the chance to turn it around.

Having been dominated in the first half, and fortunate to be only one goal behind, we finally began to play and compete after the break. Ironic therefore that Man City added a second just after our best spell of the match, but no one could have deserved a goal more than Beinlich did.

We pushed forward, more in hope than expectation, but got picked off on the break for 3-0. I thought it had become 4 through Gary Flitcroft, but the referee again intervened in our favour, and we were able to limit the damage to 3-0 in a game in which City looked much more like the champions of last season than the early strugglers of this one.

The result dropped us back into the bottom three on goal difference – a one or two goal defeat would have had us above the line – but there was good news too, in the form of a £400,000 cash injection from the board. I now had the potential to make our first ever million pound signing, but it was still a question of who, when, and for how much. I didn't want to rush straight out and waste it.

In the meantime, we had back to back local derbies again, and once again North Wales followed by Merseyside. And I had a selection dilemma for the Wrexham game, a half-fit Ian Bennett or an unproven Frank Lee. I plumped for Bennett, also hoping that featuring in a good win would boost his morale, and we were good to go.

Even against lower ranked opposition, home second legs always feel like a minefield if you haven't got an away goal in the first leg. It was vital we scored first, and we'd be on a knife edge until we did. Fortunately we only had ten minutes to wait for the breakthrough to come, Scott Houghton weighing in with his first goal of the season. He nearly added another on half an hour, then both Joachim and Dyer had and missed chances to extend our lead. We were 1-0 up at the end of a dominant first half, and really should have been out of sight.

The second half was a much less comfortable affair, and I did wonder if our missed chances would come back to haunt us.

Wrexham launched a late onslaught and we were hanging on a bit in the end. They never made any serious chances, but it was tense out there, far more than it should have been. But we took the win, local bragging rights, and our place in the next round. We could hardly have asked for a tougher draw than Middlesbrough away, but we'd gone there and won in the FA Cup last season, so anything was possible.

Which was the spirit we took into the home game against Liverpool, a fixture we could only ever have dreamed of before. If we did happen to see a Liverpool side here it was their reserves, either using our stadium for their home games, or sending a youthful side here for a friendly. This time it was all business.

As such, the match was another highlight-free affair, with no chances of note on either side. I could only be pleased with my side's professionalism and spirit, and it was a sign of the respect we're now earning, that Liverpool didn't go gung ho for the win, and nor did they seem to see the draw as being a disastrous result. Conversely, it was an excellent point for us, with the only downside being that results elsewhere kept us consigned to the bottom three.

But we'd get a chance to lift ourselves out with our next match, and last of the month, at home to Nottingham Forest. It was a game I had to see as winnable, since this was a side that had finished below us last season, and who we'd already beaten twice at home in this calendar year, once en route to promotion from Division One, and again as part of that run to the FA Cup semi-finals.

After a bright opening, I thought Paul Stephenson had given us the lead on 17 minutes. He got behind the defence, and slotted what looked like a precise finish past Tommy Wright, but it just slid by the wrong side of the post. And on half an hour Forest were given a penalty, and Stan Collymore, our nemesis from last season, stepped up to smash it home and give Kharine no chance of reprising his Arsenal heroics. 1-0 to Forest.

The ref ruled in their favour again when David Phillips took Scott Houghton out of the game with an ugly hack. It looked a certain red to me, but he was let off with a mere booking, and we trailed 1-0 at half time. And although we had almost constant possession and pressure in the second half, that was how it stayed, with particularly disappointing performances from Bruce Dyer and

Julian Joachim. This was a hurtful defeat, and one which made survival seem a very long way off.

Chapter 6 – November:

The Nottingham Forest result convinced me that major changes were needed; incomings and outgoings at both ends of the pitch. I moved in the transfer market for a striker I'd been tracking for a few weeks: Mark Sale, Bradford City's tall target man and poacher, who'd been on incredible form in Division Three. I hoped and believed that he could continue his run for us, and as our front pairing had only scored three goals all season between them, it was well worth the gamble and the quarter of a million pound outlay. The plan was for him to take Bruce Dyer's place in the side, for now, but to sell Paul Stephenson, who at 29 years old wouldn't hold his transfer value forever. I listed him at £900,000, but would happily take three quarters of a million for him.

Also transfer listed was Liam Daish, who was having a disappointing season for me, and didn't have much room for improvement at 28 years of age. But he was still a first team regular, and an established international, so I placed him on at £1.3 million, although I would be happy to accept any offer that ran into seven figures. And I wouldn't be rushing out to buy a replacement; the position would go to Don Hopkin as soon as Daish vacated it.

As for the rest of our transfer kitty, I had been mentally earmarking it to make the Kharine signing a permanent one, but his performances had begun to tail off, so I was holding fire on that. A lot would depend on Ian Bennett's performance against Middlesbrough in the League Cup tie, for which Mark Sale and the two loanees would be unavailable. It was the first of a double header, with the league fixture following immediately afterwards.

We battled well for 38 minutes in the first game, but when a chance fell to the excellent Craig Hignett, I knew he were in trouble. He skipped round Bennett and slotted home neatly to give them the lead. But we could have had an instant reply, Houghton with a great opportunity, but he lacked Hignett's composure and spurned the opening. 1-0 to Boro at half time.

I thought we could fight our way back into the game, but Middlesbrough dominated after the break, and I had to admit it was perfectly well deserved when they added a second. However, just when I was resigning myself to our fate, the goal was chalked off for a handball I hadn't spotted, and we had hope again.

I chose this time to make the attacking substitution to try and capitalise on our reprieve, Joachim coming on for Thomson, a reshuffle, and players instructed to push forward. But it was to no avail, Boro still looked the most likely scorers, and I had no complaints about our 1-0 defeat.

On paper, we had a stronger line-up for the rematch, but you couldn't see it on the pitch. Boro dominated again, Bradley Allen should have given them the lead in the first half, but Nicky Mohan finally did, and I couldn't see a way back into it for us.

Into the second half, Brendan O'Connell added a deserved second for them, but then Andy Curtis pulled one back out of nowhere from nothing, and suddenly, unexpectedly, we had hope again. But as we gambled in pushing forward for the equaliser, they picked us off on the break, twice, and we went down to humbling 4-1 defeat. Pointless again, and damage to the goal difference we could ill afford too. I should have shut up shop when we went 3-1 down.

I can remember nothing about the next game, other than we lost 1-0 at home to Chelsea. I do remember offering our biggest ever win bonus, but during the game running out of ideas, giving up, and realising that I could not keep this side in the Premier League. It was what everyone had said ever since we clinched promotion, but it still hurt, deep inside, in a way I couldn't understand and had never experienced. I was in a seriously dark place, worried about my mental health, and ready to hand in my resignation. Instead, after a chat with the chairman, I decided to stay on, and prepare for life in the division below, while still hoping for a miracle that would keep us up. I cut the wage bill by loaning Des Seaman to Bournemouth and selling Frank Lee to Yeovil. I also transfer listed top earner Scott Houghton, and made everyone else outside the first team available for loan.

Next match was Wimbledon away and we were taking an absolute pasting for 29 minutes, 2-0 down and it could have been more. Long term plan or not, this was too painful for me to cope with, and again, I decided to hand in my resignation after the game. But in the space of two crazy minutes, former Chester man Aiden

Newhouse scored a freak own goal, and Andy Curtis weighed in with an equaliser, and we were somehow level at half time.

I still couldn't let myself believe, but clearly the players did, and on the hour Paul Stephenson nipped in to give us the unlikeliest of leads. 3-2, against all odds, but still so long remaining …

As expected, Wimbledon pushed forward, but we soaked it up, and caught them on the break – 4-2! Mark Sale's first goal from the club! And an incredible, unbelievable 4-2 away win after being 2-0 down. It was indeed a funny old game.

There was another six goal thriller in our next match. Graham Hyde gave Norwich the lead against us in the very first minute, but once again we came roaring back, and we were going goal crazy all of a sudden – three of them before half time, from Scott Houghton, Paul Stephenson and Liam Daish. All transfer listed players, ironically.

But we couldn't hold the lead. Former Chester man Colin Woodthorpe pulled one back, and Spencer Prior equalised to break our hearts. I was not enjoying this season, not one little bit. Even getting performance of the week for the Wimbledon win couldn't console me, especially after Notts County beat Middlesbrough to increase their lead over us.

Still, these results had made me reconsider throwing the towel in on our survival chances, and with six pointers against Bolton and Notts County coming up, our next three games were crucial. And after a visit to the children's ward at the Countess of Chester hospital, where the kids, some of whom might not even see another Christmas, were so excited to have Premier League footballers delivering their presents, along with Father Christmas himself, of course (aka, me in the suit!), both me and the lads were more determined than ever to keep us up there. So I brought Tony Thomas and Dimitri Kharine back for additional loan spells, after their initial ones had expired, and they would feature in the home game against Leeds.

Chapter 7 – December:

Our clash with Leeds was a grim, hard fought one for a long time. Andy Curtis and Mark Limbert both had absolute shockers and were replaced at the interval. My half time team talk was more about winning for the sick kids than anything clever or tactical, but it struck a nerve with the players, and they went out ready to sweat blood and lay everything on the line. We forced ourselves into the game, but it took a freak own goal from Bryan Small to put us ahead. Leeds had to chase the game, and their doing so allowed us to pick them off on the break. Mark Sale should have scored, but Deryn Brace and Paul Stephenson actually did, for a magnificent 3-0 win. It was worth another performance of the week award, our third of the season, and more importantly, I was once again energised, engaged, and invested in our bid to avoid relegation. The only downside was that Notts County won again, but we were now within three points of not just them, but also Spurs, Arsenal, Chelsea, and Norwich. And Notts County were up next, for our biggest game of the season.

It was, as you might expect, a tense, tight game. But Paul Stephenson, who was really finding form, gave us a first half lead, and we fought like lions to retain it. It was far more gritty than pretty, but it got the job done, a crucial 1-0 win which saw us leapfrogging not just County, but Arsenal and Spurs too, and moving level on point with Chelsea. These London heavyweights weren't sides you'd expect to stay down there, but the more sides between us and the drop zone, the better.

The last game before Christmas was also away, against Bolton, and even though I was starting to feel festive, the celebrations would be curtailed if we lost that. I found it ironic that I was being tipped for Manager of the Month, when I had basically downed tools and phoned in the job half-heartedly for much of it. But I was back in the right headspace now, and looking to lead this club to its greatest ever achievement. There was also an FA Cup run to think about, having been drawn away to Carlisle in the third round, a tie which had the worrying possibility of our becoming the first Premier League side to be knocked out by a non-league one.

There were Santa hats in the crowd at Burnden Park, Shakin Stevens, Slade, and Wizzard playing over the tannoy. But we were in no mood to spread any festive cheer Bolton's way, and instead we took them apart with both precision and passion, with Deryn Brace, Andy Curtis, and Paul Stephenson grabbing the goals in a commanding 3-0 win which earned us yet another performance of the week award, and more importantly, some breathing space over the bottom three. It was also the perfect lift for the squad ahead of our Christmas party.

The lads who were out on loan came back to join the rest of the squad for the night, which was nice, and gave me a chance to recap on how they were doing. Des Seaman had only been at Bournemouth for a few weeks, and had struggled a bit on his two appearances to date, but he was always going to be a long way from the first team, and it was about long term development for him really.

So too for Steve Harrison, still only 17 (needless to say, I made sure he stuck to the soft drinks on our night out) but he was getting regular football at Yeovil, albeit out of position at right back. It wasn't ideal, and I sympathised, but I loved that he was knuckling down and showing such character and determination there. He'd also notched his first career goal during his 13 appearances to date as well.

At 25 years old, and after three seasons as a first team regular, things were a bit different for Nicky Southall. He wasn't there for experience or development, or even to prove himself really; we knew what he could do. But he was far enough down the pecking order for it not really to be worth having him kicking his heels and pulling in his recently increased wage. As expected, he'd proven to be one of Kettering's star players, making the number eight shirt his own in the heart of midfield, and notching a couple of goals and a couple of man of the match awards during his 18 appearances there. That said, he'd not done anything spectacular to suggest he could play in the Premier League; if we went down and sold players, he'd come back into contention, but if we stayed up, I'd probably list him for a permanent transfer next season.

The most successful loan, by far, and the most meteoric rise was that of Don Hopkin. Last season I thought little of him, and had Steve Harrison ahead of him in the pecking order after his arrival. But his meteoric rise had begun with a superb pre-season, and now he was playing brilliantly for Leyton Orient, forming a rock solid partnership with Adrian Whitbread, getting his first senior goal among his 18 appearances, and doing enough to force his way into the England Under-21 side. I didn't put pressure on him by telling him so just yet, but as soon as a place in our first team opened up, I would recall him from the loan and throw him straight into the starting eleven.

Needless to say, a great night was had by all. Mostly we all stayed together as a unit, although there was inevitably going to be some kind of splitting off into factions based on age and life situation. Most of us present were young single men in their early twenties, who were just coming to terms with being minor celebrities, and they spent much of their night enjoying the attentions of attractive young women. I was mostly having a drink and a laugh with Gritty, my assistant Paul Brown and the rest of the coaches, and Mick Gooding who was the same age as me and an absolute gem of a pro. He'd accepted his playing days were over, and had taken on a new unofficial role as a mentor to the younger lads, and a de facto assistant coach. Slightly more mature players, family men like Liam

Daish, Paul Stephenson and Dimitri Kharine eventually gravitated to us as well, realising, perhaps reluctantly, that they were now at a stage in their lives where they had more in common with us lot than the likely lads on the dancefloor practising their smoothest moves and best chat up lines.

I found a little time for myself, I made sure of that, and snuck outside for some fresh air, and to think about things. I pondered just how close I'd come to giving this all up, to walking away from these lads, this team, this city, all of which I loved so dearly. I thought about how when I was at my lowest ebb, when all the fight, and hunger, and self-belief were draining out of me, these lads stood up, and stepped forward, and dug deep within themselves to fight for me, for us, against all the odds. And I thought of the kids at the hospital, so delighted, so excited to see me, to see us, and how they were fighting their own battles, far bigger than anything I had ever faced, but they didn't let it get them down, they didn't let it leech away at their love for life. And for the first time, the very first time ever, I allowed myself to fully consider, to fully embrace the magnitude of what we had achieved here, what we were continuing to achieve here, for this club, this city, and the wonderful, resilient, witty and welcoming people therein. And I don't mind telling you I had a little cry. And I don't mind telling you it turned into a big cry. And I don't mind telling you I'm crying again as I write this now.

I don't know how long I was out there in the cold night, but long enough for me to be missed anyway. Fittingly, it was the skipper Andy Curtis who took it upon himself to come out and bring me back. He saw me there, and didn't need to ask what I was thinking, and I didn't need to say anything, because he just knew. I think we all knew.

"Come on in for a dance, boss," he said instead. "Everyone's on the floor now, even Joycey's having a go! And the chairman's wife made Stevie Harrison dance with her, and he looks absolutely terrified!"

I nodded, and got up. Yeah, I felt like I could bust a move or two right then. And if young Neil Joyce, who was nursing a broken rib and so heavily strapped that he had to wear a shirt two sizes up, could get up there, so could I. After strutting my stuff upright for a couple of songs, we all had to sit on the floor instead, rocking and swaying as the DJ played *Oops Up Side Your Head* by The Gap Band. Needless to say, we and all the fans present changed the lyrics, chanting instead, "We are Premier League, say we are Premier League!" And we were. And I would do everything I possibly could to make sure we stayed that way.

I had a lovely Christmas Day with my family, and I think it's fair to say my son was spoiled rotten by a bumper crop of presents this year, and then it was on to a Boxing Day clash with surprise league leaders Blackburn, who after seemingly having had the heart ripped out of their team by summer departures, were arguably exceeding expectations just as well as we were.

The narrative arc would be immensely more satisfying if we pulled off another upset win in front of the Bank Holiday crowd, but the truth is Blackburn were just too good. But it was unexpected source who did the damage: Ashley Ward, who had been plying his trade just down the road at Crewe, came into the first team from nowhere for his first Blackburn appearance, and scored two of their goals in a 3-0 win. It was a result which was reckoned to have cost me the Manager of the Month award, and Blackburn boss Kenny

Dalglish didn't get it either, despite their continuing tenure at the top of the league. Instead it went to Brian Horton at Man City, who had streaked up the league from being relegation battlers to title contenders between the clocks going back and Christmastime.

As for me, I had a big homecoming to look forward to. When the fixture list came out there was some chagrin amongst the fans that we'd been give a New Year's Day fixture away to Southampton, but it was fantastic for me personally. It meant I could sing *Auld Lang's Syne* with my family and oldest friends for the first time in years, and it was in its way as joyous and meaningful as the Christmas night out with the team. Although as dyed in the wool Saints fans, most of my hosts stopped short of wishing me luck for the next day's game, and those who did, did so through gritted teeth.

Chapter 8 – January:

And so to New Year's Day at The Dell; I had a lot of great, treasured memories from here. I'd celebrated goals by the likes of Ron Davies (also a former Chester City player!), Mick Channon, and Bobby Stokes. Oh, Bobby Stokes! And when the song started echoing around the stadium, *When The Saints Go Marching In*, I had to check myself and bite my lip to refrain from singing along.

But this was more than just a nostalgia trip of course, and we weren't just there to make up the numbers. We'd had some memorable trips down south: Arsenal, Millwall, Wimbledon, and found ourselves on a tremendous run of three successive away wins. If we could muster a fourth, it would take us towards the dreamy, heady heights of mid table respectability.

I mentioned Davies, Channon, and Stokes, but the new hero around here was Matt Le Tissier. I loved the way he played, I loved his loyalty to Saints, but he disgusted me in this game, spitting at Mark Limbert when he thought he'd been fouled. I couldn't believe he escaped with a yellow card for that, nor that Andy Porter did for a horror tackle on Scott Houghton that took one of our best players out of the game. Less than half an hour gone, and I already felt that Southampton should have been down to nine men, and my disgruntlement increased exponentially on 35 minutes when Southampton took the lead with an incredible 30 yard rocket from rookie full back Chris Stewart.

Nicky Banger should have extended the lead immediately after the break, but missed his chance, and we still had some hope. I brought Joachim on, and we had a handful of half chances in our late onslaught, but no clear opportunities. We were back to the 1-0 losses, and looking nervously over our shoulders once again. Very nervously when we learned that Spurs, Arsenal, and Notts County had all won, and with Houghton out for six weeks with his injury, we were reinstalled as odds on favourites for the drop. Le Tissier came into our dressing room after the game, apologised to Limbert, and they shook hands. It was a nice gesture, but scant consolation for the predicament we were in danger of falling back into.

Our league position meant that some people were calling our next match a must win game, which was all well and good, except that it was against Man Utd, the biggest club in the country, arguably the world, and unbeaten away all season!

As both of our wide midfielders, Tony Thomas and Deryn Brace, were also full backs, I instructed them to track back and mark Lee Sharpe and Ryan Giggs, the most dangerous wing pairing in the Premier League. But the move backfired as early as the third minute, with United right back Chris Wilder, freer now to get forward, scoring to give them the lead. Already, my game plan was out of the window, and we had a mountain to climb.

On 19 minutes, it took Dimitri Kharine at his very best to deny Jan Aage Fjortoft from scoring United's second. We were hanging on by his, and our fingertips. But we saw it through to half time, consolidating but without forging any meaningful chances, until on the hour mark when I decided to go for broke, bringing on Julian Joachim and throwing men forward. But it was to no avail, slumping to yet another 1-0 defeat, and it felt like we were as far from survival as we had been before that incredible pre-Christmas turnaround.

It was onto FA Cup action next and a much-changed side. Steve Lomas joined Scott Houghton for a long spell on the treatment table, the on-loan players were unavailable, and it meant a start for Julian Joachim, and a place on the bench for Bruce Dyer. If Nicky Southall hadn't been out on loan, he would have been in the squad; I'd think about whether to recall him or anyone else after the game.

We found Carlisle's blood and thunder 4-2-4 formation and ultra-long ball tactics hard to deal with, and their right winger gave then the lead on 12 minutes. Deryn Brace could have given us an immediate equaliser, but missed his chance. But the leveller came from behind him on 34 minutes, Andy Thomson coming forward to crack home a crisp low drive. We were enjoying almost uninterrupted possession, and although we couldn't turn it into a half time lead, I felt much better about the game than I had early on.

The game followed the same pattern in the second half, only with Bruce Dyer having come on for Mark Sale. But my worst fears were realised 14 minutes from time, when Carlisle found a second, completely against the run of play. We were heading out, in the most humiliating fashion.

But we threw men forward, and Paul Stephenson was our saviour, bundling home a suitably scrappy goal with ten minutes remaining, and it was at this point that I decided I'd be quite happy with a replay at the Deva Stadium. And even as we pulled back, it worked in our favour, catching them on the break and adding a third through Alexei Poddubski. Crisis averted!

A 3-2 win then, and we were drawn at home to Leicester in the 4th round. It was a winnable fixture, and raised hopes of another long cup run, but before that came around we would have two crunch games against the north London pairing of Spurs and Arsenal, although I still couldn't quite see them a six pointers: Notts County, Millwall, and Bolton were the sides we needed to finish above.

We played really well in the first half against Tottenham, and it was an injustice when Nick Barmby fired them into the lead. It almost got worse when Gordon Durie was denied a second by Kharine, but we got the goal we deserved when Tony Thomas brought us level right on half time. Both loan players were giving us one last gift in the final game of their respective spells, but I was minded to bring at least one of them back on a permanent basis.

Spurs pushed forward in the second half, and we looked to hit them on the break. I thought it had paid dividends fifteen minutes from time, but Paul Stephenson's nerveless finish was sadly pulled back by an offside flag. It stayed 1-1, a good point for us, and in all honestly it was the least we deserved. But it was devalued somewhat when we saw that Notts County had found a shock win over Man City – their second of the season! – to go above us.

County's improvement had been based on the very successful signing of Chris Armstrong from Crystal Palace, and I now accepted that I had to spend as well. With the loan periods having expired, I had gaps to fill in goal and on the left of midfield, and I was ready to take steps to fill them.

Firstly, between the sticks, Kharine had to be the man. I negotiated a fee off just over half a million with Chelsea, a bargain I thought, although I knew his wages would be a burden if we went back down. So we would have to do everything we could now to make sure that didn't happen.

At the other end of the pitch, I feared we were lacking a bit of pace, flair, and creativity, so I moved for Trevor Sinclair from QPR, who had all three in abundance. I snapped him up for just over a quarter of a million, which would be money very well spent if he helped keep us up. I still had enough funds for one significant transfer and one loan spell, and I was more than ready to use them.

We welcomed Arsenal to the Deva Stadium, knowing that defeat would drop us into the bottom three. So we could ill afford a poor start, and it was a cruel irony therefore that Kharine's first act as permanent keeper was to pick the ball out of the net, Paul Merson skipping round him to slot the ball home in the very first minute. Cue 77 minutes of tension, high endeavour, few chances, until Stephenson again popped up with the crucial goal, just as the game was entering its final stages. Arsenal brought on a third striker, we brought on Julian Joachim to lead the counter attacks, but it finished 1-1, keeping the Gunners third from bottom, and us just above.

Trevor Sinclair was cup tied for the FA Cup game against Leicester, so I brought in his former QPR teammate Julian Joachim to play against the club where he began his career, with Alexei

Poddubski moving to the left, and Graham Potter and Bruce Dyer filling the bench. There was no thought of substitutions though, as we dominated the first half, albeit without finding the breakthrough. But it came early in the second half, with Deryn Brace finally breaking the deadlock. Leicester tried to mount a comeback, but we always had them at arm's length, and the eventual 1-0 scoreline was somewhat deceptive, because I felt that we'd won more comfortably than the result suggested.

Unfortunately, we were given a daunting fifth round draw away to Blackburn, but even that wasn't as daunting as our first game of February, away to Newcastle, who had replaced them at the top of the Premier League.

Chapter 9 – February:

Iain Jenkins pulled up with a minor injury on the eve of our game at Newcastle, so Graham Potter slotted in, with a half-fit Scott Houghton taking his place on the bench. We almost took a shock lead inside the first 20 minutes, but Mark Sale, who had so far failed to provide the goals I was hoping for, missed the opportunity. Thankfully Andy Cole was similarly wasteful for them, missing two such chances, although the second, which hit the post, was mightily close. We went in goalless at half time, but knowing we had a perilous second 45 minutes still to survive.

Newcastle continued to press, Alex Mathie was the next to miss a great chance, but then, ten minutes from time, Andy Curtis played in Deryn Brace for a deft finish to give us the lead and send the travelling fans into wild celebration. Inevitably though, Newcastle launched themselves into a late onslaught, and we were just two minutes from an incredible victory when Steve Potts denied us it with his equaliser. 1-1, still a great result, but we couldn't help ruminating on what might have been. At least the point lifted us above both Everton and Notts County.

Millwall were up next, so we went from away to the top team to home to the bottom team, which was easier on paper, but a whole different set of pressures: this was a game where a draw simply would not do.

For half an hour we produced a display of flawless dominance. Mark Limbert gave us an early lead, Paul Stephenson extended it against his former club, and then he seemed to have made it three, but for a baffling unexplained disallowance. The reprieve galvanised Millwall and they had the upper hand as we approached the interval. They seemed to have pulled one back, but the referee brought it back for a free kick to them, having failed to play the advantage. It was harsh on Millwall, but it seemed in this case that two wrongs *did* make a right.

Andy Curtis added a third soon after half time, to snuff out any chance of a comeback, and we could enjoy the remainder of the game from there. There was still time for Paul Stephenson to come close again, for Mark Sale to get a much-needed goal harshly disallowed, and for Liam Daish to finally add the well-deserved fourth goal. A 4-0 win, our biggest of the season, and a very welcome confidence boost.

We had a cup date with Blackburn next, and although we had a relegation battle to fight, I was still all in and try and win it. We produced a solid first half performance, and deserved to be going in level, but the referee bought an obvious dive from Steve Redmond, and Brian Deane converted the spot kick. That was how it stayed, an injustice in a way, but even I couldn't deny that Blackburn had been by far the better side. I was happy to see the back of them, after three defeats this season and no goals scored.

After the game I got a couple of surprise transfer bids. I let Mick Gooding go to Portsmouth on a free transfer, to maybe get a few more games before his retirement. And West Brom came in with a £600,000 bid for Bruce Dyer, which I unequivocally rebuffed. He was having his first difficult season, but he was still only 20, and had a massive future in the game.

But it came as a timely reminder that the transfer deadline was looming, and this was my last chance to strengthen. I also didn't know who'd be moving on, and would need replacements, so I had to bring players in proactively. I brought defender Guy Butters in on loan from QPR, the third player I'd signed from them this season, and paid £270,000 to Brentford for Scottish attacking midfielder Paul McDonald. Both went onto the bench for the local derby six pointer against Everton.

We started brightly, with both Trevor Sinclair and Scott Houghton coming close inside the opening ten minutes. But on half an hour Andy Curtis showed them both how it's done with a perfectly struck 25-yard rocket into the top corner and in off the bar. A brilliant goal!

We got another goal ten minutes into the second half, just as good, this one screeching into the back of the net from the boot of Mark Sale. Get in! 2-0! It was an excellent derby result which picked up yet another performance of the week award, although Newcastle's 9-1 demolition of Millwall must have been close. And the win gave us vital breathing space over Arsenal, Notts County and Everton, and also saw us climb above Nottingham Forest and Chelsea.

There were two transfer deadline bids received, both of which I rejected. Another £600,000 offer for Bruce Dyer was a no-brainer to dismiss out of hand, but the £800,000 bid for Paul Stephenson was much more tempting. Indeed, it was an offer I would have accepted earlier in the season, but he was on fantastic form, was our main scoring threat, and his goals might well prove to be the difference between survival and relegation. For the remainder of this season at least, he was still a Chester player, and a very important one at that.

Where we'd just made our first ever half million pound signing, and spent a million in total over the last couple of weeks, a national newspaper ran a feature on us, and the signings I'd made, making the point that we were the least expensively assembled squad in the Premier League. It made interesting reading for me too, as I looked over the dealings and fees that I'd long since forgotten. Especially those from my first season: Bruce Dyer for £40K (my first and maybe my best, despite his current difficulties), Ian Bennett for £70K, Graham Potter for £50K, Andy Thomson for £70K, Nicky Southall for £30K, and Liam Daish for £80K. All still here! And the only other permanent signing from that season was also still around, albeit in a different capacity: Steve Gritt, who'd signed for £8K and post retirement was now coaching the youth team prospects.

Season two saw the arrivals of Alexei Poddubski for £110K, and Paul Stephenson for £200K, along with a few small priced veterans in for the short term.

Last season, along with the short-lived Vinnie Jones spell, I also picked up Scott Houghton for £340K, Steve Harrison for £8K, Deryn Brace for £200K, Andy Curtis for £250K, and Steve Lomas for £110K.

Throw in this season's signings, Julian Joachim for £190K, Des Seaman for £20K, Mark Sale for £250K, Kharine for £520K, Trevor Sinclair for £260K, and Paul McDonald for £270K, along with free transfer Iain Jenkins, and homegrown Mark Limbert, Don Hopkin, Ian Jackson, and Neil Joyce, and it meant that our 24 man squad had been assembled at a cost of around £3 million. That actually sounded like a lot of money to me, but then again, that was pretty much what Blackburn had paid for Brian Deane alone. It was also a somewhat bloated squad now, and I'd have to sell players next season, whichever division we were in. For now though, they were all Chester City players, and we were all focused on the same goal. We'd take a big step towards achieving it if we could win at home to Ipswich in our next game.

I went with an unchanged side, and we looked solid, but the only worthwhile opportunity of a drab first half fell to Mark Sale, who missed the chance. But it was on the right side where we were really struggling, Deryn Brace and Scott Houghton both having poor games. I took a gamble on replacing each of them, with new arrivals Butters and McDonald respectively.

We looked the better side in the second half, and the next big chance also fell our way, but this time it was Alexei Poddubski who couldn't find the finish, and we ended up being the better side in a goalless draw. We'd have been happier if Notts County hadn't somehow won away to Man Utd, but as it was, we went into March still on a knife edge.

Chapter 10 – March:

The first game of what we laughingly called spring, while we scraped the ice off our car windscreens in the morning, was a home game against Manchester City. But we never really got going at all, and were second best through most of the match. We looked to be heading to a tame defeat at 2-0 down, with time running out, but Mark Sale pulled one back on 86 minutes to give us a glimmer of hope we barely deserved. The fans heading for the exits turned around and sat back down as we launched an onslaught looking for the equaliser, but it was to no avail.

And we really got that sinking feeling when we heard that Notts County had won again, to go above us. But as they were now seven points above Arsenal, who occupied the last relegation spot, maybe we really could stop considering County our only rivals, and accept that the Premier League could lose a big club after all. Especially as it had already happened to Spurs the season before last.

So no one in the bottom half of the table could consider themselves safe yet; the placings being Norwich in 11th on 37 points, Nottingham Forest in 12th on 36 points, their neighbours

Notts County in 13th on 35 points, ourselves in 14th on 33 points, Spurs in 15th, below us on goal difference, also on 33 points, Chelsea in 16th on 30 points, Everton in 17th on 29 points, Arsenal in 18th on 28 points, Bolton in 19th, deep in trouble on 24 points, and poor old Millwall rock bottom on 17 points, and almost certainly destined to stay right there. It was the situation everyone had expected us to be in.

The short but daunting trip to Anfield to play Liverpool was unlikely to see us add to our points tally, but we had to dig in and try and make sure we got something out of it. And although we acquitted ourselves well in the first half, that little dash of quality and composure in the final third made all the difference, as evidenced by Fitzroy Simpson's smart 20th minute finish which gave them a 1-0 half time lead. We had our moments in the second half but couldn't find the equaliser, and although we weren't at all disgraced in going down to a battling 1-0 defeat, it threatened to leave us in real peril.

Elsewhere, Notts County won again, this time over Spurs, which made them all but safe and ensured continued trouble for

Tottenham. Arsenal fell further into trouble too, with a poor loss at Bolton which kept up the Trotters' slim hopes of survival. Chelsea and Norwich drew with each other, Forest and Everton drew with each other, and Millwall pulled off a rare win, beating Wimbledon 2-1.

Nottingham Forest were one place and four points above us, but our trip there was one that we believed we could get something from. And we got off to a great start, with a typically composed Paul Stephenson finish giving us the lead after just seven minutes. But frustratingly, after nearly half an hour of our being in nearly full control, Forest scored with their first meaningful attack, through Gerald Dobbs.

We were also the better side in the second half, but without scoring again, and as the dying minutes ticked away, I was reflecting on a decent away point which could have been even better. And then Steve Stone popped up with the last-minute winner to break our hearts. I could have cried. I could have punched him. But above all I wished that somehow, we could have a chance to take revenge on Forest next season, for this most hurtful of defeats. But with Arsenal beating Blackburn, and Everton beating Ipswich, we were suddenly once again the most likely side to fall through the trapdoor.

It made our game with Middlesbrough the mother of all must wins, and accordingly, I offered the biggest ever win bonus for our club, ten grand a man. I hoped they could collect it, and it would have a positive effect, not put added pressure on. I also switched Guy Butters in to start, with Liam Daish dropping to the bench.

Guy Butters justified his selection on 19 minutes when our old nemesis Craig Hignett went round Kharine and looked set to roll it into empty net, only for Butters to sprint back and clear it off the line. It was tense and even from that point onwards, until Middlesbrough gambled by sending on an extra striker, losing a defender with less than ten minutes remaining. Normally in these circumstances I'd look to cover their attacking move with a defensive one, but I wasn't sure that a single point was enough anymore, so I pushed Paul McDonald forward to also give us three up front. All or nothing then, and with three minutes left it was … ALL! Scott Houghton with the most priceless goal he'll ever score, and me forgetting myself, jumping around like a lunatic on the sideline, and then suddenly remembering I was the manager, not just a fan, and waving back all my attacking players to protect that lead at all costs. And when the final whistle blew, the players ran to the dugout and I took my place amid this human scrum of celebration, yes, but a myriad of other emotions besides. We all knew how big this one was.

Other big results coming in: Bolton beating Southampton, Chelsea beating Leeds, Everton beating Millwall, Norwich beating Notts County, and in a massive North London derby, Spurs beating Arsenal. It left the Gunners five points adrift of safety, as unthinkable as their relegation was.

Chapter 11 – April:

The penultimate month of the season would begin with a battle of Stamford Bridge as we went to play at Chelsea. With both of us holding a handy lead over 18th placed Arsenal, a draw might inch both of us closer to safety, but the incentive for a winner was to open a near unassailable gap to the danger zone.

For 45 minutes it looked like we were playing out a pre-agreed draw, but then the referee gifted Chelsea a decidedly dodgy looking penalty. I fancied Dimitri Kharine to mark his return there with another penalty save, but Kevin Campbell had other ideas, and smashed it past him to give Chelsea a 1-0 half time lead.

We huffed and puffed to no avail against Chelsea's stubborn five man defensive line, and the minute we made a formation change to chase the game harder, they hit us on the break for a second, and it finished 2-0. A disappointingly flat performance, when we really needed better.

It was with some trepidation that I watched the other results coming in, but I must confess to punching the air when I saw that

Arsenal had lost at home to Ipswich. Meanwhile, Millwall's loss to Norwich meant they were the first side definitely relegated.

As for ourselves, our next game was at home to Wimbledon, the side against whom our incredible 4-2 win from 2-0 down breathed life into what was looking like a hopeless season. I felt like we needed three points just as badly here: Arsenal's next two games were against Notts County and Millwall, and I could see them winning both.

I made a few changes for the visit of the Crazy Gang, one enforced due to Butters going back to QPR, but also dropping Trevor Sinclair to the bench, moving Poddubski to the left, and bringing Paul McDonald into centre midfield. I almost removed Sinclair from the squad entirely, since Graham Potter could cover both that position and left back, where Iain Jenkins had just endured a poor game. But in the end I felt that if the game was on the line, and I needed someone to bring on to change things in our favour, Trev was much more likely to be our man. I also set the maximum ten grand win bonus again; this was no time to be scrimping on rewards.

We played through an even first half, albeit with Houghton and Curtis looking a little off form, and I was giving them each ten minutes in the second half to show improvement, or I would take them off. But before that ten minutes had elapsed, Andy Clarke had given the Dons a 1-0 lead.

I made the change immediately, Trevor Sinclair on for Andy Curtis, with Poddubski moving into the centre, and everyone looking to press forward. And Poddubski it was who brought us level with a fearsome left foot drive. All square, and it was a game of stick or twist – I chose to keep everyone pressing forward to go for the win. However, after Wimbledon threw two extra men up front, I moved to provide cover at the back, albeit with Trevor Sinclair and Paul McDonald bombing forward on the break to try and give us all three points. But it was Wimbledon who came away victorious, Scott Fitzgerald's last-minute winner casting a gloomy, ominous shadow over the Deva Stadium. Arsenal had beaten Notts County, Bolton had beaten Chelsea, and we were right back there in the mire. Ironic that the opponents who had first lifted us out of trouble had dropped us right back in it again.

It was a quick turnaround to a tough away fixture at Norwich, who boasted an excellent home record, but with Arsenal, to my mind, certain to move onto 37 points, we simply had to get something out of the game. I dropped Scott Houghton to the bench, with Andy Thomson coming in at right back, and Deryn Brace pushing further forward into right midfield. He would give us more solidity, and he'd also scored some very useful goals from there, plus I always backed players going back to their former clubs. But we didn't start the game well, and ten minutes in, the nightmare scenario, Les Ferdinand giving them the lead.

Paul McDonald had a great chance to bring us level seven minutes later, but wasted the chance. I felt like I was aging another year with every minute that passed. I was steeling myself for the half time break, and any changes I could make to turn it around. But we collapsed badly in first half injury time, with both Ian Woan and Chris Sutton netting, but amazingly, both goals were (probably wrongly) disallowed. We could and should have been sunk, but somehow there was still hope.

Brace was having a poor game against the side where he'd served his apprenticeship, and I brought Scott Houghton on his place. And he set up Paul Stephenson for a great opportunity on 53 mins, but our most reliable finisher wasted the chance when it mattered most. Two minutes later though, his strike partner Mark Sale showed him how it was done, getting on to Paul McDonald's through ball to fire us level. Get in!

Norwich went all out attack with four up front. Having consigned Millwall to relegation, it looked like they wanted to do the same to us. But in doing so they left the right side open, and I brought Trevor Sinclair on to hopefully exploit that space. The next big chance fell to Ferdinand again though, but thankfully this time he blazed it over.

I had my heart in my mouth throughout those unbearably tense late exchanges. I wanted the win, that wasn't to be, but at least this time we avoided the agony of another late winner against us. We came off to see that Arsenal had won, but that was nothing we hadn't expected, and it was now Spurs occupying third from bottom, albeit just one point behind ourselves and their local rivals.

Our last game of April was away to Leeds: not necessarily a game where you'd expect us to get a result, but frankly, we couldn't afford not to. I switched Houghton and Brace, but otherwise went with an unchanged side.

We endured the mother of all nightmare starts against Leeds, going 2-0 down inside ten minutes through goals from Frank Strandli and Rob Bowman. I was just about ready to go into damage limitation mode, when Mark Limbert crashed home an excellent volley, and we were back in the game. 2-1 to Leeds at half time.

Steve Howey added a third early in the second half, and then right at the end, Gary Speed capitalised on a Limbert error to make it 4-1, a very harsh scoreline on us I felt, but that didn't matter: at this stage of the season a loss is a loss.

Speaking of which, Arsenal won again – it looked like they were completing a great escape. And results elsewhere were better: Bolton were held to a draw by Ipswich, Notts County lost to Millwall, and Spurs lost to Newcastle. We would go into May above the relegation zone, and with two home games against fellow strugglers Notts County and Bolton still to come. We would have snatched your hand off for such a scenario at the start of the season.

Chapter 12 – May:

Despite our heavy defeat to Leeds, I still felt like that eleven and bench was our best, and most balanced and adaptable line-up for the visit of Notts County, in what could conceivably be called the biggest game in our entire history.

    We seemed prone to poor starts of late, and we let Neil Lewis in for a great chance with only two minutes on the clock, but thankfully Dimitri Kharine blocked his finish. And just five minute later, Paul Stephenson demonstrated how finishing should be done, with an exquisite lob over Lee Butler to give us a priceless lead. On 23 minutes Scott Houghton looked to given us a massive boost towards survival, beating Butler with composure and poise, only for the goal to be ruled out for a supposed foul on the defender. I hoped that moment wouldn't come back to haunt us. But our confidence wasn't dented, and just three minutes later Poddubski was given a similar chance, produced a similar finish, and this time it counted! 2-0!

    All we needed was professionalism, but a stupid moment of carelessness from Liam Daish allowed Neil Lewis in, and this time he produced the finish to put us deep in danger again. Another goal might be enough to send us down.

But cometh the moment, cometh the skipper! Andy Curtis, with a brilliant strike, 3-1, and pandemonium in the stands as the fans lurched from one emotion to the other. There were still scares ahead; Chris Armstrong on 81 minutes coming close, denied by Kharine when he could have set up a very uncomfortable finale. But we saw it out for an emotional 3-1 win. All attention to the final scores now: by my reckoning, unless Spurs had managed to win away to title-chasing Man City, we were staying up!

It came in … Man City 3, Tottenham 1! Survival! And with a game to spare!

Some fans began streaming on to the pitch in celebration around me. The stewards move to block them off, but instead I blocked the stewards, pulled them away to allow the fans passage, then turned to the stands and began waving everybody else on. It was irresponsible I know; I'd most likely be fined for it, and rightly so, but right then I didn't care. I just wanted to share the moment with as many people as possible: players, fans, and hey, even opponents. County's fans and players were celebrating too, since the Spurs result kept them in the Premier League as well. Both sets of fans were on the pitch, dancing and singing side by side, congratulating one another and making pledges to meet up for the return fixtures next season. It was a wonderful moment, one of the best I'd ever known in the game, and it was a long moment too. We were an hour on the pitch after the game before everybody eventually filed away, to continue their celebrations in the pubs, clubs, and bars, or at home with their nearest and dearest. There wouldn't be an open top bus parade this time around, but in my opinion, surviving a season in the Premier League was an even greater accomplishment than getting there in the first place.

There was, as you might expect, a carnival atmosphere for our last game of the season. Quite literally in this case though, because apparently I'd pledged to sing *I Will Survive* on the pitch if we stayed up. I had no such recollection of making this promise, but was told it happened at the Christmas party. It was a long old night, the details of which got increasingly hazy as it went on, and enough witnesses confirmed that they saw and heard me make the pledge for me to think there might have been something in it. And so, man of my word that I am, I agreed to karaoke the song before kick-off against Bolton. So far so quirky, but some cheeky wee scamp at the club (my money's on Andy Curtis) notified the local and national presses, and embellished the story that I'd be singing in full disco gear. Needless to say the story got around, and soon was the talk of the town, in fact the country. This had gone too far really; I wasn't sure such antics were appropriate, and it seemed especially disrespectful to Bolton, who were playing their last game before relegation. I compromised by saying I'd only do it for sponsorship, if we could raise £10,000 for the children's ward at the Countess of Chester Hospital. Soon, everyone was talking about that, it was in all the papers and TV, and it even went on that new world wide web thing, and we reached the target five times over. So there I was on matchday in a shiny skin tight jump suit, murdering a disco classic in front of 5,000 people. And was I nervous about doing this? Well, at first I was afraid. I was petrified …

  Weirdest thing was taking my place in the dugout, dressed as I was. At least lots of fans in the crowd were also thus attired, and even some Bolton fans, putting a brave face on relegation, had followed the theme. And when I approached Ossie Ardiles for the pre-match handshake, I noticed he was wearing a big pair of Elton John glasses. Of course, Ossie himself had already been on Top of the Pops, with Chas 'n' Dave that time, so my musical exploits were small fry to him.

All fun and games then, but we still had a match to win, and I was serious about taking the three points. I'd rested a few players, who were one card away from suspensions that would carry over into next season, but it was hardly untried rookies I was putting in: Graham Potter, Bruce Dyer, Trevor Sinclair, with Julian Joachim and Steve Lomas on the bench. But Paul Stephenson was the star of the show, producing a finishing masterclass in the first half, to put us 2-0 up with his 13th and 14th goals of the season, and as the minutes ebbed away, those goals always looked like being the difference between the two sides. And so it proved with the victory lifting us above Chelsea into a highly respectable finishing position of 14th place in the Premier League, seven points above the drop zone in the end. No one could say we didn't deserve to be there.

We took a well-earned lap of honour at the end, and even some of the Bolton fans stayed to applaud us. Ossie congratulated me on our achievement; in turn I said I hoped they came straight back up, and I genuinely meant it. But the showmanship wasn't over yet, and the chairman had massive plans to steal the show.

He took a microphone and spoke over the tannoy, beginning by congratulating me and the players on staying in the Premier League, then thanking the fans for their continued support, all the things you'd expect. But then he dropped the most beautiful bombshell, in his own special way:

"Ladies and gentlemen, fellow Cestrians, what a day to celebrate, what a season to celebrate! It's the sort of occasion you'd love a souvenir from, isn't? And I think you should take ... the seats you've been sitting on today! Because you won't need those anymore. This summer we are going to replace those ... with sixteen thousand new ones!"

There was a mixture of spontaneous cheers and stunned silence, before everybody settled down to listen to him continue. "Yes, it's true folks. Jason and his backroom team have built a squad fit for the Premier League, and in return, I am going to give you a stadium fit for the Premier League! This lovely little ground which has been our home for the last few years will continue to be so. We will play right here, *but* – it will be rebuilt, redeveloped and above all, expanded! This was a home designed for lower league football, and as such it was fine, but we are not that side anymore. We're Premier League! And having survived a season at this level, and proved we deserve to be here, I want to give us every opportunity to continue to do so, long term, with a facility fit for purpose, and a capacity which allows us to welcome everybody who wants to be part of this club's adventure, and to come as close as we can to competing financially with the rest of this division. I am under no illusions about this – I know we will still be the poor relations in this league. I know we will still be a minnow in shark infested waters. But we are not content to remain small fry – this new, redeveloped stadium will be a sign of our growth. This fish is getting bigger and bigger!"

He paused again, for breath as much as dramatic effect. "And you might be wondering, where will we play in the meantime? Who can we ground share with? Tranmere?"

The crowd booed.

"Crewe?"

They booed again.

"Wrexham?"

This one drew the loudest boos of all, by far.

"There is no need for that nightmare scenario, ladies and gentlemen. Because this hasn't been a snap decision on our part. The planning began as soon as we got promoted, and the project was confirmed as soon as we clinched survival in this division last week. We have contracted the best in the business, the fastest in the business, and they have guaranteed that the redevelopment will be complete in time for next season!"

The crowd cheered, as loudly as they would for a goal.

"And finally," added the chairman after the noise died down, "I can confirm that the funding for this product has come from a combination of the directors' personal fortunes, private sponsorship, Sports Council grants, and the City of Chester itself. Nothing at all will come out of Jason's budget for player transfers and wages; we want to continue to grow on *and* off the pitch. So take your souvenirs, tell all your friends, and we will welcome you and them back here next season, when we will be able to accommodate more of you than ever before!"

*

I read up and found that wasn't strictly true: we'd had a crowd of over 20,000 at Sealand Road once. But that wasn't all-seater like this one would be, so it that sense, yes it would be Chester's greatest ever stadium, including the ancient Roman amphitheatre, as evidenced by the architect's plans and artist's impressions which circulated around the media over the next few days. I just hoped that we could fill it, and play a brand of football which was both entertaining enough for our new fans, and successful enough to keep us in the top division.

Time to rest and recharge would be invaluable therefore, but before we could hit the beaches for the summer, one of our squad still had some football to play: Don Hopkin's loan spell at Leyton Orient was ending with them competing in the playoffs. It would give him a chance to feature in yet another promotion campaign, and to make his first appearance at Wembley.

Things couldn't have gone better for the O's in the semi-final, as they smashed Cambridge 9-1 on aggregate, 5-1 away in the first leg, and 4-0 at home in the second. So Hopkin did indeed get his Wembley appearance, but it would end in disappointment, with his side narrowly losing 1-0 to Grimsby in the final. But his performance on the day was a good one, and I suspected he'd get to play there again one day. And he didn't need to worry about missing out on promotion to Division One, because I knew for a fact he'd be playing in the Premier League next season, as would all of us. Because we'd earned the right to be there, and would never stop fighting, never give up, no matter what. Our redeveloped stadium would be no Wembley, but we would play there with as much pride as if it were.

Because we were Chester City. We were Premier League. And yes; at the end of the day, when the battle was won: we *were* having a laugh. And we didn't want to stop laughing any time soon.

Printed in Great Britain
by Amazon